Little Owl's Day

by Divya Srinivasan

VIKING

An Imprint of Penguin Group (USA)

Chikit-chikit-chik!
A squirrel was chittering loudly.

Little Owl could sleep no more.
He blinked open his eyes.

Too bright to be moon,
this must be . . .
"Sun!" he whispered.

"Little Owl," yawned Mama,
"go back to sleep."

But Little Owl was wide awake!

Wrens were trilling sweetly.

The ground was covered in flowers
Little Owl had never seen. Their petals
were open for the sun and the bees.

"Moths!" Little Owl called.
But no, these were butterflies.

Little Owl thought he knew the forest well,
but it seemed so different now.

Dragonflies were skimming the pond.
They even flew backwards!

Little Owl couldn't wait to tell the bats.

Snakes slid into the water,
gliding among lilies and reeds.

Turtle was sunning herself on the rocks.

The meadow erupted with barks and yips.
Wolf pups were at play!

Their mother howled, and the pups
dashed off to meet her.

Near Grumbly Cave, there
was Bear, splashing after fish!
"You're always asleep," Little Owl said,
"when I want to show you the moon!"

"You're always asleep," Bear said, "when
I want to show you a rainbow. Come."

Little Owl had never been to the waterfall.

At sunset, Little Owl started home.

Deer bit blackberries from thorny branches.
Boars were rooting around the brambles.

A piglet squealed, "Little Owl is awake!"
"Hello, Little Owl!" squealed another.

The possums were only just stirring.

Hedgehog was still sleeping, so mice feasted on mushrooms.

Stars began to glitter as the sky went dark.

The moon was rising.

Little Owl reached his tree.
A bunny nodded a sweet "good night"
and ducked into her burrow.

Little Owl was astonished. She lived just below!

Little Owl was excited to tell Raccoon all about his day. Then he had one more place to go.

Little Owl was sleepy, but . . .

he had promised Bear he'd
show him the moon.

USA * Canada * UK * Ireland * Austr.

First published in the Unite
an imprint of Penguin

Copyright © 201

Penguin supports copyright. Copyright fuels creat
diverse voices, promotes free speech, and cre
culture. Thank you for buying an authorized edition o
and for complying with copyright laws by not reproc
scanning, or distributing any part of it in any form with
permission. You are supporting writers and allowing Penguin
to continue to publish books for every reader.

LIBRARY OF CONGRESS CATALOGING-
IN-PUBLICATION DATA
Srinivasan, Divya, author, illustrator.
Little Owl's day / by Divya Srinivasan.
            pages cm
Summary: Little Owl explores the forest at daytime
after being woken up by a noisy squirrel.
ISBN 978-0-670-01650-1 (hardcover)
[1. Owls—Fiction. 2. Bedtime—Fiction.
3. Forests and forestry—Fiction.
4. Forest animals—Fiction.] I. Title.
PZ7.S77414Lg 2014   [E]—dc23
            2013047053

Manufactured in China

1 2 3 4 5 6 7 8 9 10

Book designed by Nancy Brennan
Set in Sassoon Infant